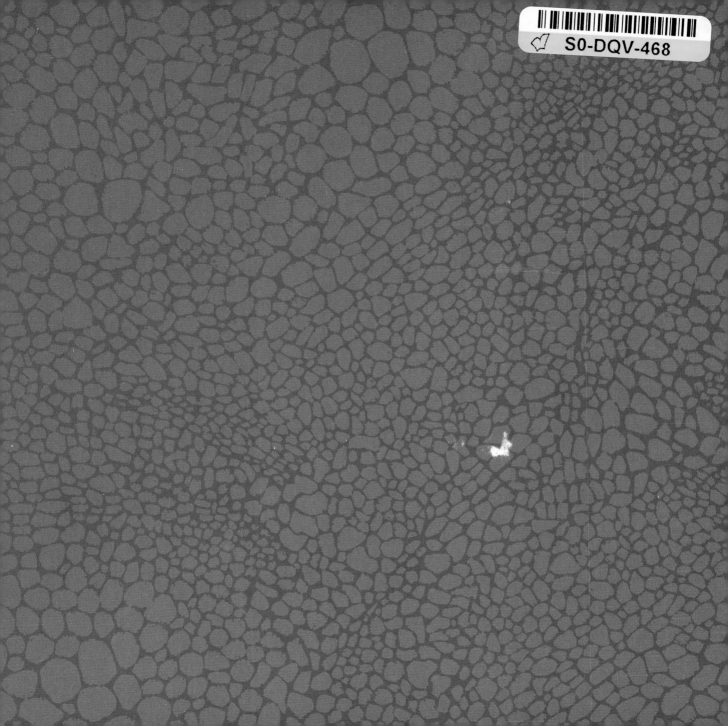

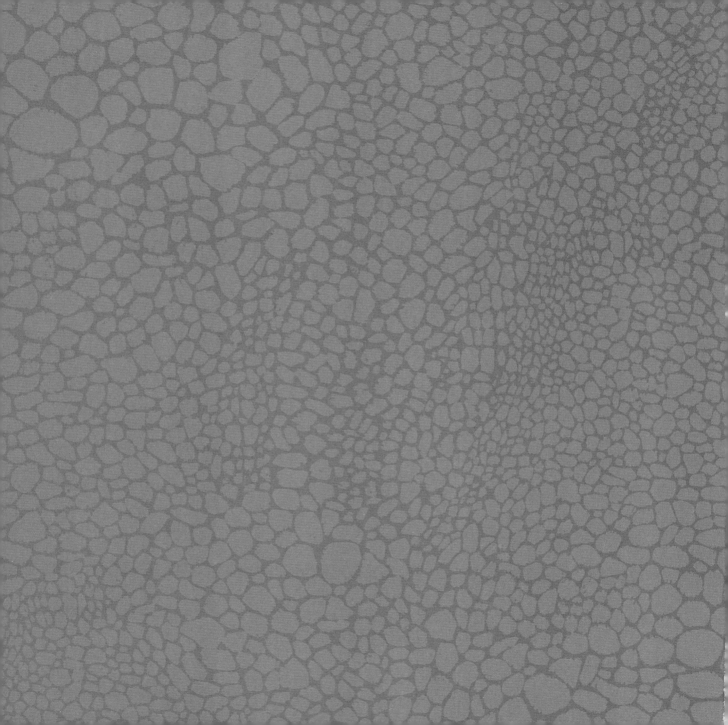

Disney · PIXAR

THE GOOD DINOSAUR

Read-Along
STORYBOOK AND CD

This is the story of two unlikely friends named Arlo and Spot. You can read along with me in your book. You will know it's time to turn the page when you hear this sound. . . . Let's begin now.

For information address Disney Press, 1101 Flower Street, Glendale, California 91201.
Printed in the United States of America
First Paperback Edition, October 2015
First Hardcover Edition, October 2015
1 3 5 7 9 10 8 6 4 2
ISBN 978-1-4847-5099-5
FAC-038091-15240

For more Disney Press fun, visit www.disneybooks.com

Disney PRESS
Los Angeles • New York

SUSTAINABLE FORESTRY INITIATIVE   Certified Sourcing
www.sfiprogram.org
SFI-00993
This Label Applies to Text Stock Only

At the base of Clawtooth Mountain lived a family of farmers. The smallest one was named Arlo.

From the moment he was born, Arlo was scared. Poppa even had to coax him out of his egg! "Come on out."

Arlo worked on the farm with his brother and sister. As his siblings grew older, they earned the right to make their marks on the family silo. But Arlo's fear held him back, and he struggled to find his place. Even simple chores terrified him. Years passed, and a gap was left on the silo as Arlo continued looking for a way to make his mark.

One night, Poppa nudged Arlo into an open field. "Okay, now take a walk out there."

As Arlo nervously stood in the darkness, a bug landed on his nose. "Poppa. Poppa."

Poppa gently blew on the bug and it lit up. It was a firefly! "Sometimes you gotta get through your fear to see the beauty on the other side."

Poppa brushed his tail through the tall grass. A swarm of fireflies rose up, flickering their lights.

Arlo was delighted. "Wow!"

Arlo and Poppa ran through the grass, leaving a glowing trail in their wake. The two watched together as fireflies rose into the air, making beautiful arcs of dancing light that twinkled against the sky.

The next day, Poppa frowned at a pile of corn scattered around the silo. Something was getting into their harvest! "I've had it up to my snout." He gave Arlo an important job. "*You* are gonna catch that critter."

This was Arlo's chance to make his mark!

Poppa and Arlo built a trap, and then Poppa left an eager Arlo to protect the silo. But when the trap rattled, Arlo froze. The critter inside looked hurt. Arlo felt sorry for the critter, so he opened the trap. "Okay . . . you're free."

When Poppa found out that Arlo had set the critter free, he was not happy. He knew Arlo had to get over his fear or he would never make his mark. "We're gonna finish your job right now."

Poppa and Arlo went off to find the critter, following its tracks into the wilderness.

Arlo was nervous. "But, Poppa, what if we get lost?"

"As long as you can find the river, you can find your way home."

As they searched, a storm hit. The ground trembled, and a surge of water roared toward them. Poppa threw Arlo to safety but couldn't save himself. The flood swept him away, and he disappeared into the river.

With Poppa gone, life on the farm was hard. Winter was approaching, and the family had to get the harvest in.

Arlo was determined to help. "Don't worry, Momma, I won't let us starve." He put a load of corn on his back and carried it to the silo.

When Arlo arrived at the silo, he was surprised to find the critter inside, chomping on a corncob. Seeing the critter made Arlo angry. "My poppa would still be alive if it weren't for you!"

Arlo chased the critter to the river, trying to get the corncob back. The critter startled Arlo. Arlo jumped back, and they both fell in the water!

The current pulled Arlo farther and farther from home. He gasped for air and tried to stay afloat. "Help—Momma! Momma! MOMMA!"

The river tossed Arlo about, turning him around and around until he didn't know which way was up. Suddenly, the water swept Arlo toward a huge boulder. *Bam!* Everything went black.

When Arlo opened his eyes, he found himself on a sandbar in the middle of the river. He heard a howl and looked up. The critter was looking down at him from a ridge.

Arlo struggled out of the river and up the ridge. By the time he made it to the top, the critter was gone.

Arlo looked around. Nothing seemed familiar. "Where's home?"

Then he remembered Poppa's words: *As long as you can find the river, you can find your way home.*

Frightened and alone, Arlo walked back toward the water.

As Arlo followed the river, it started to rain. He tried to build a shelter. From their burrows, creatures laughed as the rain poured in on Arlo.

Arlo was shivering in his shelter when the critter appeared, carrying a stunned lizard in its mouth. The critter dropped the lizard in front of Arlo, offering it to him as a snack. When Arlo showed no interest, the critter fetched a giant bug. Arlo was disgusted!

Next the critter brought Arlo some berries. Arlo devoured them and tried to get the critter to find more. "You know . . . *nom, nom, nom.*"

Arlo followed the critter as it sniffed out a berry tree. Suddenly, the critter started to growl. There was a snake in the tree! The critter protected Arlo and chased the snake away.

Just then, a voice came from the woods. "That creature protected you. Why?"

Arlo frowned. "I don't know."

Hidden among the trees was a mysterious *Styracosaurus*. He wanted the critter to protect *him*!

Arlo was not so sure. "W-wait, he—he's with me."

The *Styracosaurus* meditated for a moment and then opened one eye. "I name him, I keep him. Mmmm . . . Killer!"

Arlo tried to name the critter, too. "Grubby!"

"Lunatic!"

"Spot!"

The critter looked up at that, so Arlo said the name again. "Come here, Spot!"

Spot pranced over to Arlo, and the two ran off.

Arlo and Spot walked on, playing along the river. Spot even taught Arlo how to swim! That night, Arlo and Spot found themselves in a field of fireflies. "Spot, watch this!"

Arlo brushed his tail through the grass. Hundreds of fireflies rose into the night sky. Spot loved it.

Watching the fireflies made Arlo think of Poppa. "I miss—I miss my family."

Spot looked confused. He didn't understand what Arlo was saying.

Arlo tried to explain. He made little dinosaur figures out of sticks. Then he drew a big circle around them. "Family."

Spot studied the figures. Then he fetched more sticks and made three human shapes. He laid two of them down and covered them with dirt. He was showing Arlo that his family had died.

Arlo covered his figure of Poppa with dirt, too. Thinking about Poppa made Arlo feel sad. "I miss him."

The two friends sat next to each other and howled at the sky. Then they curled up and went to sleep.

The next day, there was a terrible storm. Scared, Arlo ran from the lightning. It reminded him of the storm in which he'd lost Poppa. When the rain cleared, Arlo and Spot realized they had lost sight of the river. Soon a group of pterodactyls appeared. The beasts attacked and tried to capture Spot.

"No! Spot!" Arlo put his friend on his back and ran as fast as he could. Overhead, the pterodactyls chased after them. "Help!"

Hearing Arlo's cries, some *Tyrannosaurus rexes* headed toward the friends! But instead of attacking Arlo and Spot, the *T. rexes* fought off the pterodactyls.

The *T. rexes* were looking for their herd of longhorns. Arlo made a deal with them. If Spot could find the herd, they would lead Arlo to a watering hole where he could ask for help.

"Come on, Spot. Sniff it out, boy."

Spot followed the scent to the longhorns: raptors had taken them!

Arlo was frightened, but he and Spot helped fight to get the herd back. For the first time, Arlo had a reason to be proud of himself.

That night, the *T. rexes* shared stories around a campfire. Arlo couldn't believe how brave they were. "I'm done being scared."

The biggest *T. rex* looked at Arlo. "Who said I'm not scared?"

"But you took on a croc—"

"And I was scared doing it. Listen, kid, you can't get rid of fear. But you can get through it. You can find out what you're made of."

Arlo had never thought of fear that way.

Suddenly, a snowflake drifted by Arlo's nose. "The first snow."

Winter had arrived. Arlo knew he had to hurry home.

The next day, Arlo helped the *T. rexes* drive their herd. When the longhorns started to drift away, Arlo roared at them. As he used his tail to help keep the animals in line, he saw something familiar in the distance. "There it is . . . Clawtooth Mountain. There's home!"

Arlo and Spot said good-bye to the *T. rexes* and headed toward the mountain.

The two ran all day, chasing birds and jumping over boulders along the way. As the sun began to sink, the two climbed high above the clouds and watched the sunset together. "Wow."

At last, the friends reached the base of Clawtooth Mountain. They howled with excitement.

Someone howled back! In the distance, Arlo saw a human figure. Spot was curious, but Arlo scooped him up. "We need to get home."

That evening, another storm hit. High above, pterodactyls circled. They dove down and grabbed Spot! Arlo tried to get him, but he tripped and fell into a tangle of brambles. "Help me." As Arlo struggled to break free, a rock tumbled down the cliff and hit him on the head.

Knocked unconscious, Arlo dreamed of his poppa. "Come on, Arlo. We gotta move."

But Arlo knew he couldn't leave Spot behind. "Spot needs me, so I gotta go help him. Because I love him."

Poppa smiled. He knew Arlo had it in him. He told Arlo to go take care of the critter.

Suddenly, Arlo woke up. Determined, he broke out of the brambles and took off to find Spot.

The pterodactyls had Spot trapped inside a dead tree by the river. Arlo used all his strength to scare away the pterodactyls.

As a flash flood crashed toward Spot, Arlo jumped in front of him. A wall of water hit the friends.

Arlo tried to swim toward Spot, but the rapids were too strong. Arlo couldn't reach him. Worse, the friends were being pulled toward a giant waterfall! Arlo grabbed Spot just as the water pushed them over the falls.

The two rose to the surface. Arlo looked at Spot, unsure if his friend was okay. Spot wearily opened his eyes. Arlo had saved his life!

Relieved and exhausted, Arlo closed his eyes and took a deep breath. They had both made it.

The rain had stopped and the sky was clear. The friends climbed to
the top of a ridge. Looking down, they could see the farm! Arlo and Spot
were happy to be close to the end of their journey. "We're home, Spot!"

Suddenly, someone howled. The human figure Arlo had seen earlier
appeared. The man was soon surrounded by his family.

Spot approached the group curiously.

Arlo watched as they circled Spot, rubbing his head and smiling.

Spot hopped back up on Arlo's back, but Arlo nudged him toward the family. He drew a circle around them, as he had with the family of stick figures. He knew Spot was home.

The friends tearfully hugged, then sadly howled to each other as Spot and his family walked into the woods together.

Alone again, Arlo walked through the Clawtooth Mountain pass to his family's farm. Momma looked up from her work in the field and saw him approaching. *"Arlo!!!"* She ran to him and hugged him tightly.

With tears of joy, the family embraced Arlo, happy to have him home.

Later Arlo stood next to their silo. As his family watched, he proudly placed his mark right next to Poppa's.

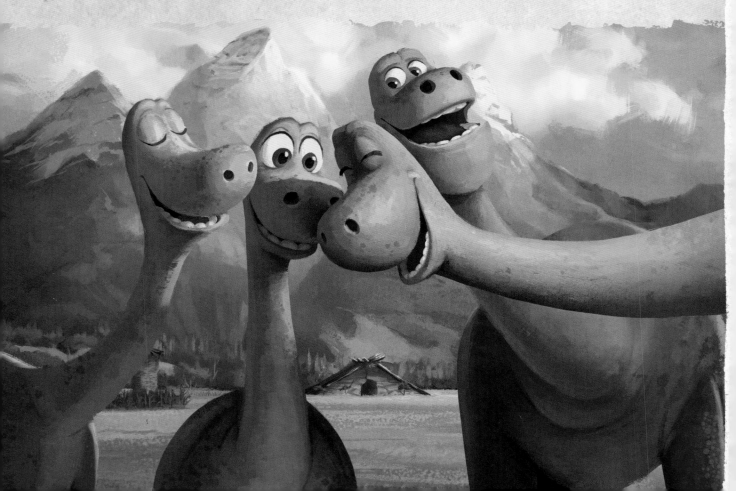

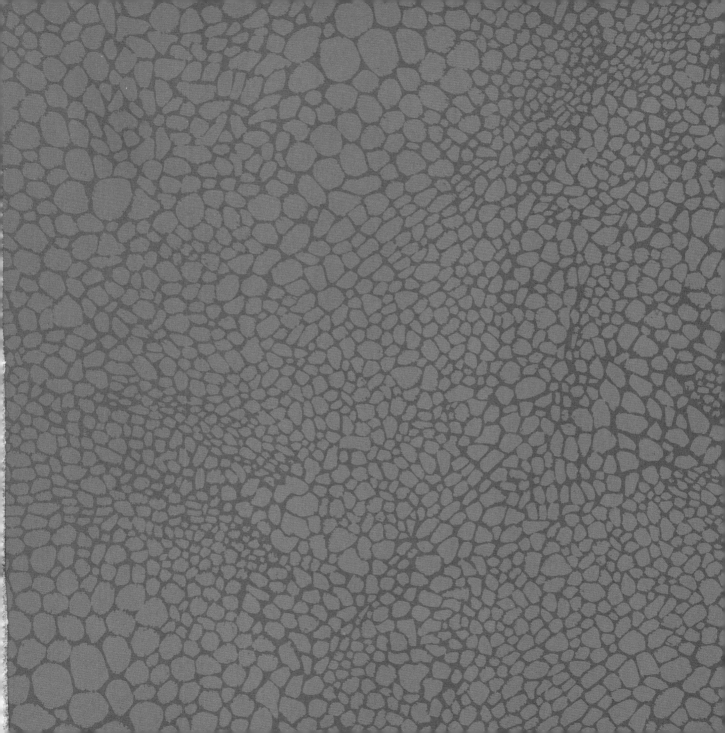

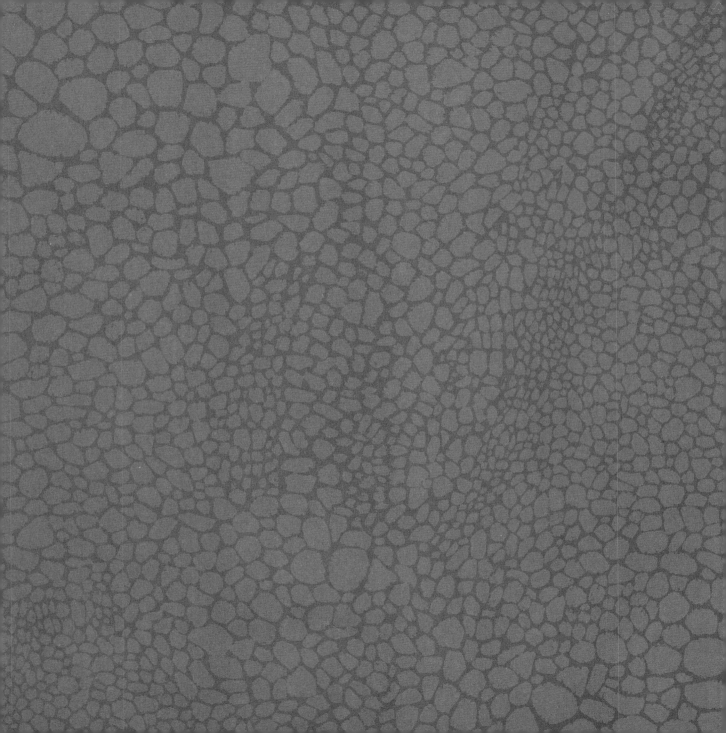